GRANDMA'S TWO

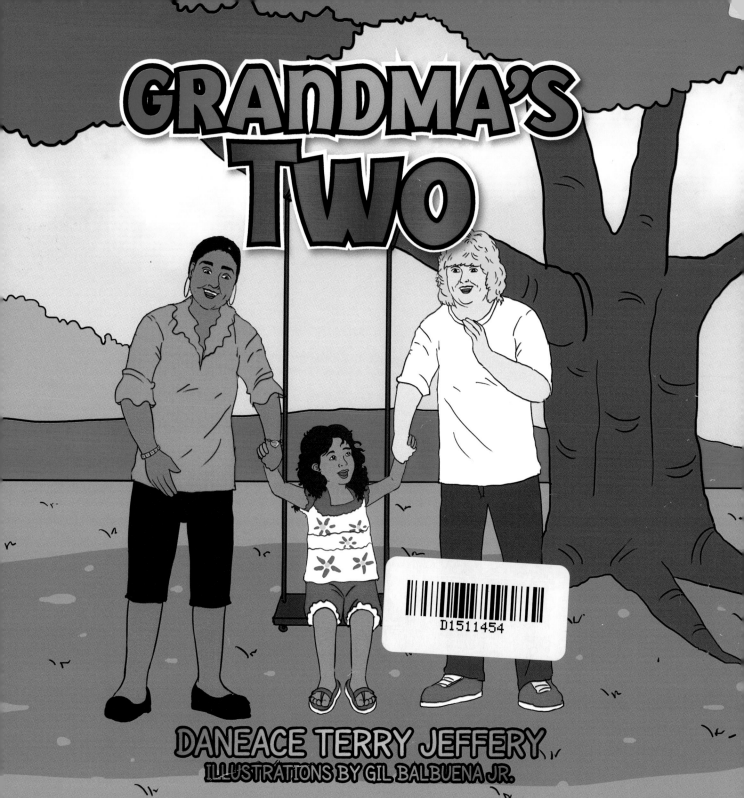

DANEACE TERRY JEFFERY
ILLUSTRATIONS BY GIL BALBUENA JR.

Rev. date: 07/21/2014

To order additional copies of this book, contact:
Xlibris LLC
1-888-795-4274
www.Xlibris.com
Orders@Xlibris.com

DEDICATION

To Alena, Khloe, Khadijah and Nusaybah,
may your life be filled with joy and happiness.

Visiting my two grandmothers is so much fun. They both love me and we do many things together.

One grandmother lives in a big city and the other grandmother lives in a small town.

I call my Mommy's mother Grandma and I call my Daddy's mother Nonnie.

What name do you call your grandmothers?

When I visit Grandma in West Virginia; it takes a long time to get there.

We drive past cornfields,

farms,

cows,

horses,

and into another state. Then we drive up into the mountains. While Daddy is driving, sometimes I fall asleep.

Grandma and Granddad own an outdoor sporting goods store. Many hunters come to the store to buy supplies. When I am at the store, Grandma lets me help the people find what they need.

The hunters come in and tell stories about hunting and fishing.

I quietly listen to their stories, just like my Grandma. She says it's important to be a good listener, work hard, and be respectful.

On Sundays we go to church. Grandma plays the piano and leads the people in singing. She has a pretty voice and I try to sing just like her. Grandma and Granddad have lots of friends who always play with me after church.

Some of the people in church are the same people who come into the store,

so everyone knows my name.

Back at Grandma's house, she lets me help her make dinner. I stand on a stool so I can reach the counter. Grandma says I'm too young to stand near the stove. One day, I'm going to be old enough to stand at the stove and help her cook.

On Sundays, Grandma cooks a big dinner. Aunt Gigi and Uncle Jared also come over to eat. My Grandma makes the best chicken and dumplings and I am learning how to be a good cook

just

like

her.

When it's time to leave I am very sad. I have so much fun working and playing with my grandparents that I never want to leave. I hug Grandma really tight, hoping I don't have to go. I never want the fun to end. But Mommy and Daddy tell me I can visit another time.

When I visit Nonnie in Baltimore, we don't have to drive very far. Nonnie is a teacher and lives in a big city. Nonnie doesn't have a big yard to run and play, but we still have fun together. It's very different at Nonnie's house than it is at Grandma's.

But I get excited when I get to spend the night.

Nonnie lives near a big park and we can walk there to play on the swings and sliding board.

She pushes me really high on the swing and I feel like I'm flying, higher

and higher, and higher.

There are lots of other kids in the park to play with too. We all laugh together. Nonnie makes us a special picnic lunch with my favorite fruit,

blueberries!

She also packs peanut butter and jelly sandwiches. We bring a blanket to sit on while we eat.

Nonnie tells me stories about our family. Stories about my Daddy when he was a little boy make me laugh.

The thing we all enjoy the most when I'm with Nonnie is going to the circus. There are a lot of exciting acts going on at the same time.

Nonnie buys me cotton candy that

melts in my mouth…and on my hands.

The clowns do funny tricks that make me laugh. The elephants are soooo big, but I am not afraid of them. There are pretty dancing girls that dance around the floor. Some of them even ride the elephants. There is only one part of the circus that scares me… fireworks. They hurt my ears and make me jump.

I DON'T LIKE FIREWORKS!

There is so much to do and see when I visit my grandmothers. They are different, but alike in many ways.

They both teach me about

Love,

Respect,

Family,

Working hard

And having Fun.

I love to sleep over and spend special times with them. Sometimes we do the same kinds of things, like cooking, reading books or playing outside.

But what makes my life so special is the difference between my two Grandmothers.